Walt Disney's CLASSIC
Pinocchio

Adapted by Eugene Bradley Coco
Illustrated by Ron Dias

A GOLDEN BOOK • NEW YORK
Western Publishing Company, Inc., Racine, Wisconsin 53404

Once upon a time, long ago, the wishing star shone brightly in the night sky. Its beams formed a shimmering pathway to a sleepy little village below. Only one house still had a light burning in the window, and that was the workshop of Geppetto, the kindly old wood-carver. Geppetto was happily finishing a puppet he had made out of wood.

"The only thing left to do now," said Geppetto to the puppet, "is to give you a name. Let's see...I shall call you Pinocchio!"

"What a grand name for such a handsome boy!" Jiminy Cricket said with a chirp.

That night, as Geppetto lay in bed, he looked out at the bright evening star and made a wish. Geppetto wished that Pinocchio were a real boy. Then he drifted off to sleep.

Suddenly the Blue Fairy appeared in Geppetto's workshop. "Good Geppetto," whispered the fairy, "you have given so much happiness to others, you deserve to have your wish come true." Then, with a wave of her wand, the Blue Fairy brought Pinocchio to life.

"A-a-am I a REAL boy?" Pinocchio asked the Blue Fairy.

"No, Pinocchio," she answered. "First you must prove yourself brave, truthful, and unselfish. You must also learn to choose between right and wrong. Your conscience will help you."

"What's a conscience?" asked Pinocchio.

"That's the small voice that people don't always listen to," Jiminy Cricket answered.

The Blue Fairy made Jiminy Cricket kneel down before her, and she dubbed him Pinocchio's Official Conscience. It would be his job to see that Pinocchio did only what was right. Then the Blue Fairy vanished.

When Geppetto awoke, he could not believe his eyes. "My wish has come true!" he shouted. "Pinocchio is alive!" Although Geppetto soon realized that Pinocchio was still made out of wood, it mattered little to him.

"I shall love you just the way you are," he told Pinocchio. Then he explained that Pinocchio had to go to school, like all boys. And so, that very morning, Pinocchio happily set off.

Pinocchio hadn't gone far when Gideon, a cat, and Foulfellow, a sly fox, saw him.

Foulfellow thought, "A wooden boy with no strings. I'll bet Stromboli, the puppeteer, would pay a pretty price for him."

Foulfellow convinced Pinocchio that acting was the life for him and sold Pinocchio to Stromboli.

That night, after Pinocchio had performed to rounds of applause, Stromboli locked him in a cage.

"How am I ever going to get out of this horrible place?" said Pinocchio, sobbing.

Just then a voice called out, "Don't worry, Pinoke, I'll save you!" It was Jiminy Cricket! He had followed Pinocchio to Stromboli's caravan. Now Jiminy pulled, pushed, and shook the lock on the cage. But he couldn't get Pinocchio out.

Suddenly the Blue Fairy appeared. "Pinocchio, why
didn't you go to school?" she asked.

"I...uh...was brought here by a big green monster who
was going to cook me for his supper," he lied. As he spoke
Pinocchio's nose began to grow, until it was twice as long as
it had been before.

"You're lying, Pinocchio," said the Blue Fairy sadly.
"It's as plain as the nose on your face."

"Please give him one more chance," pleaded Jiminy Cricket. "I'll make sure he never lies again."

"One more chance, that's all you'll have," said the Blue Fairy. She set Pinocchio free, and he promised never to lie again.

The next day he headed straight for school. But on his way he was stopped by Foulfellow once more.

"And where are you going on such a fine day?" said the fox with a sneer.

"To school," replied Pinocchio.

"Ha! School is no place for a boy like you!" said Foulfellow, laughing. "If you follow me, I'll show you a place that's much more fun—Pleasure Island!"

"Don't go, Pinoke!" warned Jiminy Cricket. But Pinocchio did not listen, and before Jiminy knew it, Foulfellow had sold Pinocchio to the mean old driver of the Pleasure Island stagecoach. Jiminy Cricket hopped on the coach, too, so he could keep an eye on Pinocchio.

The coach was pulled by six unhappy donkeys. The coachman went from village to village, buying up all the boys he could. Once the coach was full, he raced to the ferry bound for Pleasure Island.

Pinocchio sat beside a loudmouthed boy named Lampwick. "Don't worry about a thing," said Lampwick with a chuckle. "Once we get to Pleasure Island, we won't have to listen to anyone or worry about what's right or wrong!"

On Pleasure Island, Pinocchio forgot everything the Blue Fairy had told him. He fought with the other boys, smoked a corncob pipe, tossed rocks through windows, and yelled and screamed with all his might. Then he followed Lampwick down Tobacco Lane to the Pool Hall.

"This is a great place, Lampwick!" shouted Pinocchio.

But as Pinocchio turned to his friend, he could not believe his eyes. Lampwick had suddenly grown long ears and a tail. Lampwick had turned into a donkey!

Pinocchio felt the top of his head. He, too, had grown donkey ears and a tail! Now he knew where the coachman got his tired, sad-looking donkeys.

"Come with me before it's too late!" cried Jiminy Cricket, who had been following Pinocchio.

Pinocchio and Jiminy Cricket quickly ran to the shore and jumped off the cliffs into the sea. They swam all the way back to land and rushed to Geppetto's house, but he wasn't there. Pinocchio was worried.

Just then a white dove dropped a note from high in the sky.

"It's from Geppetto," said Jiminy Cricket, "and it says that he went looking for you and was swallowed by a whale named Monstro. He's trapped inside the whale."

"I must find him!" cried Pinocchio. He and Jiminy Cricket raced back to the sea. Soon they spotted Monstro and swam as close as they could to the whale.

Suddenly Monstro opened his mouth and gulped down a school of fish. Pinocchio was swallowed along with them. Inside the whale, Geppetto was fishing, and he felt a tug on his line. When he reeled it in, Pinocchio was at the other end.

"My son! My son!" shouted Geppetto. "I thought I'd never see you again!"

"I missed you so much, Father," said Pinocchio. "I've been a bad boy and I'm sorry."

"That's all right, my son," said Geppetto. "The important thing is for all of us to get out of here."

"I have an idea!" cried Pinocchio. "We'll make a raft and build a fire! It'll make Monstro sneeze us right out."

When they built the fire, the smoke tickled Monstro's nose till he let out a huge sneeze. Pinocchio and Geppetto were sent flying out to sea on their tiny raft.

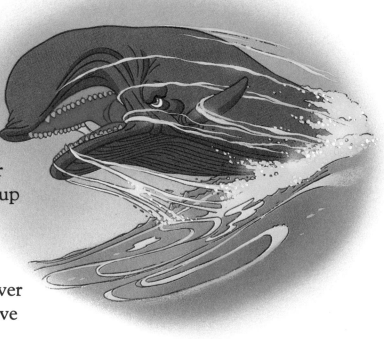

Monstro charged right after them. When the whale caught up with the raft, he splintered it with one blow of his powerful tail.

Geppetto was sinking. "Never mind about me!" he cried. "Save yourself, my son!"

But Pinocchio swam back to Geppetto and helped him to stay afloat on a piece of the raft. Geppetto was washed safely ashore, but Pinocchio didn't fare as well. Geppetto found him lying in the water among the rocks, lifeless.

Geppetto took Pinocchio home. As he wept the soft voice of the Blue Fairy filled the room. "Pinocchio, you've proved yourself brave, truthful, and unselfish. Now you will be a real boy."

Pinocchio moved his arms and legs and blinked his eyes. He was alive—and no longer wooden. Geppetto danced for joy.

Jiminy Cricket was happy, too. In Pinocchio he had sure proof that when you wish upon a star, your dreams come true!